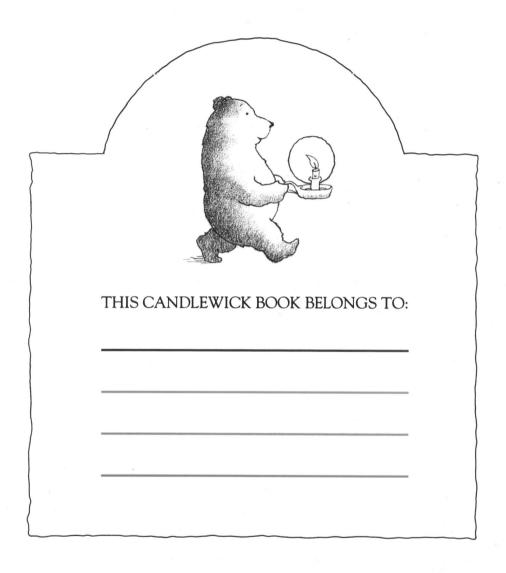

THIS CANDLEWICK BOOK BELONGS TO:

_____

BLUE WHALE
80 feet

SPERM WHALE
60 feet

DIVER
6 feet

KILLER WHALE
30 feet

FIN WHALE
70 feet

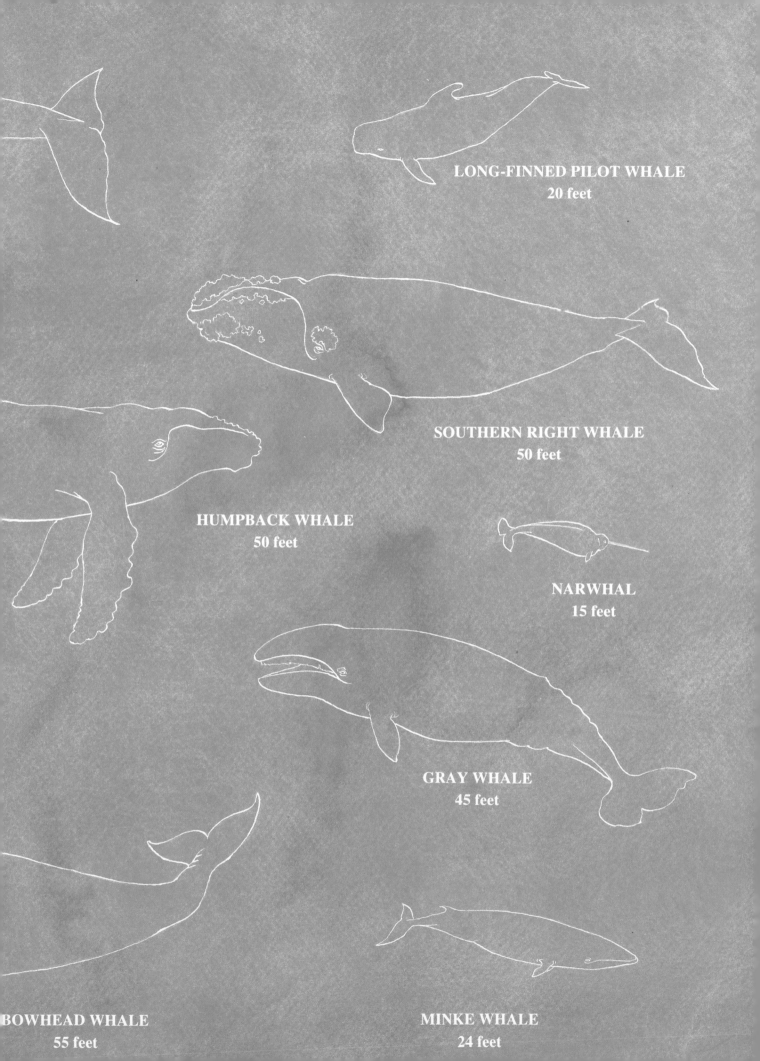

LONG-FINNED PILOT WHALE
20 feet

SOUTHERN RIGHT WHALE
50 feet

HUMPBACK WHALE
50 feet

NARWHAL
15 feet

GRAY WHALE
45 feet

BOWHEAD WHALE
55 feet

MINKE WHALE
24 feet

To everyone who has ever
done anything to try to save whales.
J.A. T.H.

The author and publisher wish to thank
Martin Jenkins for his invaluable
assistance in the preparation of this book.

First U.S. paperback edition 1994
First published in Great Britain in 1992 by Walker Books Ltd., London.

Library of Congress Cataloging-in-Publication Data

Allen, Judy.
Whale / written by Judy Allen ; illustrated by Tudor Humphries.
—1st U.S. ed.
Originally published: London : Walker Books. 1992
Summary: One night a young girl and her parents witness the seemingly
magical rescue of a mother whale and her baby that are exhausted from
trying to outswim a spreading oil slick. Includes a whale fact sheet.
ISBN 1-56402-160-2 (hardcover)—ISBN 1-56402-383-4 (paperback)
1. Whales—Juvenile fiction. [1. Whales—Fiction. 2. Rare animals—Fiction.]
I. Humphries, Tudor, ill. II. Title. III. Series: Allen, Judy. Animals at risk.
PZ10.3.A4276Wh   1993
[E]—dc20   92-53019

2 4 6 8 10 9 7 5 3 1

Printed in Hong Kong

The pictures in this book were done in watercolor.

Candlewick Press
2067 Massachusetts Avenue
Cambridge, Massachusetts 02140

WHALE

by
Judy Allen
illustrated by
Tudor Humphries

CANDLEWICK PRESS
CAMBRIDGE, MASSACHUSETTS

"I've never seen the moon so big or so brilliant," said Anya's mother, as she kept the wheel of the little cabin cruiser steady. "It's a magic night, now the storm is over."

"Good magic or bad magic?" said Anya doubtfully. She thought the moon looked fine, but she wasn't so happy about the lightning, which was still chasing itself to and fro in the distance, just where the sky became the sea and the sea became the sky.

It usually took three hours to cross the water between the island, where Anya's grandmother had her house, and the mainland, where Anya and her parents lived. Before, they had always traveled in daylight, but this time they had had to wait for the sudden, fierce storm to move on its way, and they were late.

The sea looked much deeper at night than it did in the daytime, and it also looked wider, and stronger, and stranger. It was not rough and there were no waves hitting against the bow of the boat, but there was something that Anya's father called "a heavy swell." This meant that the sea made big, slow movements underneath the boat, as if it were breathing long, slow breaths — or as if something enormous were moving just below its surface.

While Anya's mother steered the boat toward their home harbor, whose lights looked as tiny and distant as stars, her father tried to make the radio work properly. The storm had left the air full of electricity, and the words were coming out of it mixed up with sparkling noises, as though a thousand needles were being shaken in a glass box.

Anya thought she would rather listen to the clattering and scratching of the needles than to what the radio was saying. It was talking — on and on and on — about an oil tanker, which had run aground in the bad weather, and about rescue operations and a vast oil slick.

"Are people drowning?" said Anya, holding tightly to the edge of the boat and looking at the deep, dark water.

"No," said her father. "Everyone's safe."

"The people are safe," said her mother, "but just imagine what damage that oil slick will do."

Anya knew what her mother meant. A flood of oil would come out of the side of the wrecked tanker and spread over the surface of the water. It would choke the fish to death. It would stick to the wings and beaks of the seabirds so they couldn't fly or feed. It might even catch fire and send flames running across the surface of the ocean, threatening anything that was on it.

"Are we near it?" she asked nervously.

"No," said her mother. "It's a long way away."

"Oil slicks travel," said her father gloomily.

"Depending on the wind and the tides, it could come our way in a day or so."

The moon and Anya stared at the swelling sea.

"I know why people used to believe in sea monsters," said Anya. "It does look like something huge is making the water bulge up and down. Especially back there."

"It's the current," said her father, with his eyes on the radio.

"It's the pull of the moon," said her mother, with her eyes on the distant light of the harbor buoy.

"It *is* a sea monster," said Anya, suddenly frightened, her eyes on something far behind — but not far enough behind. "Something rose up just now and went down again, and it wasn't water."

"Where?" said her father.

"There!" said Anya.

"I can't see anything," said her father.

"It's not there now," said Anya in a small voice. "It might be coming closer — underneath."

"Don't panic," said her mother. "What did it look like?"

"Big and dark and wet," said Anya.

"Like the sea?" said her father gently.

"It wasn't the sea. It was different."

Anya's mother slowed the boat and let it drift a little sideways so that she could look behind them.

"Oh, there," said Anya and her father together, as a dark mass rose up through the surface of the moonlit water for a second and then sank out of view.

"Whale!" whispered Anya's mother. "It's a whale. It really is."

Anya's mother kept the engine turning gently so that the boat stayed more or less in one place, and they got out the binoculars and took turns staring at the sight that the moon was lighting up for them.

"It's a humpback whale," said Anya's father, "but it doesn't look right. It's floating and sinking, not swimming and diving."

"I think it's in trouble," said Anya's mother when she had the binoculars. "I wonder if it's injured in some way."

"There's something with it," said Anya when it was her turn.

"There's something — it's hard to see — oh — it's a small one. It's a very small one. It has a baby."

"I know what's happened," said Anya's mother, sounding as if she wished she didn't. "The tanker broke up in the breeding grounds. She's just had her calf and she's had to outswim the oil slick. She's exhausted."

"But she *will* be all right?" said Anya.

No one answered her.

"*Will* she be all right?" said Anya, wondering if she wanted to hear the answer.

"I think she may not be," said her father quietly, as the shiny curve of the whale's back slid down under the water again. The baby went down with her. "She doesn't have the strength to keep herself and her calf at the surface. Whales breathe air, Anya, like us. I think she may be drowning." He turned back to the radio.

"But can't we do something?" said Anya, horrified.

Her mother put her arms around her. "There's nothing we can do," she said, and her voice sounded as if she might cry. "She is very big and very heavy — there is no way we could support her while she rests. I think we'd better go on home."

"We can't *leave* her," said Anya, staring and staring at the place where the whale had disappeared.

"We can't help her," said her mother, "and I don't want to watch her die."

"I'm trying to get the coast guard on the radio," said her father, "just in case anyone else can do anything. But I can't get through."

The whale's back appeared again, but she did not rise as far out of the water as she had before. She was gone again, almost at once.

"She's not blowing," said Anya's mother sadly. "She's not breathing."

"I can't *bear* it," said Anya, and her voice began to get louder. "Please help her. Someone must save her. *Do* something — *please*."

The moon watched the dark swelling water.

Strange sounds began to fill the air, coming from everywhere and nowhere — trumpeting sounds, almost like elephants, but not elephants, and then strong, steady chirping sounds, almost like birds, but not birds.

"What's that?" said Anya's mother.

The sounds grew stronger. They shivered through the sky as though the moonlight had a voice. They echoed deep under the water and made the boat shudder.

"Look," said Anya. "Oh, look!"

Far behind them, and way over to each side of them,
the water was moving. Great, dim shapes were breaking
the surface, gleaming silver in the moonlight. Breathy
waterspouts were rising in glittering columns into the air.

Massive tails were flicking upwards and then sinking in slow, deep dives.

"Whales are coming!" said Anya's mother. "It must be the rest of the herd."

"I've heard of this," whispered Anya's mother, though the songs of the whales were so loud that her voice was almost lost. "I've heard of them rescuing each other."

The four whales that were acting as supporters lay still and steady on the surface. The rest swam and dived almost as if they were playing, but despite their massive size, they made no waves; the little boat did not rock.

"They're still coming," said Anya's father. "But they're not all the same kind."

Enormous though they were, they were powerful
and streamlined, and they surged through the water
at astonishing speed.

"We should get into shore," said Anya's father
dreamily. "They could sink us." But he didn't move.

"Yes," said Anya's mother, but she didn't move either.

Anya said nothing — she just stared and stared as the
nearest whales submerged and then rose again, slowly,
steadily, lifting the mother and her calf between them.

The moonlight showed humpback whales with long flippers and tiny back fins, the smooth backs of great right whales, the huge, blunt head of a sperm whale, and, in the distance, a basking blue whale, so vast that it looked like a small island. There was even a narwhal with a single corkscrew tusk, like a sea unicorn.

"I don't understand," said Anya's mother.

Something else was odd, too. As the whales moved in the water, the moonlight showed great, dark gashes in their sides. Some of them even had harpoons buried deep in their bodies, the shafts sticking out at odd angles. Every one of the whales that surrounded the female and her calf was badly injured — but not one of them seemed to mind, not one of them seemed affected by its wounds.

"This is the strangest sight anyone ever saw," said Anya's mother.

"This is magic," said Anya.

Afterward, none of them could say how many whales they saw that night, and none of them could say how long it was before the female humpback recovered, but they all agreed on one thing: In the very second that she began to move on, in the very second that she no longer needed help — every single one of the other whales vanished. They didn't swim away, they didn't submerge, they just weren't there anymore, and where their songs had been, there was silence.

When they reached land, Anya and her parents asked
everyone they knew, and a lot of people they didn't know,
if they had seen what had happened. No one had.

"We're the only ones," said Anya's mother, "who know
that the spirits of the dead whales came to help her."

Later, there was a report on local radio: A female
humpback whale and her calf had been sighted,
swimming strongly towards the south, well away
from the spreading oil slick.

"We're not quite the only ones who know,"
said Anya. "The whale and her baby —
they know, too."

WHALE FACT SHEET

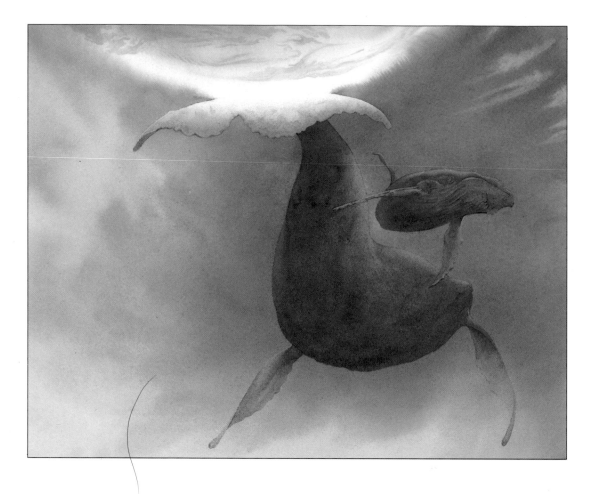

There are many different kinds of whales, including the eighty foot long blue whale, the largest animal that has ever lived. They are found in seas and oceans all over the world, but are now most numerous in the cold waters of the Antarctic. All the different whales have been greatly reduced in number and some, such as the blue whale and the northern right whale, are now very rare and may become extinct. Others, like the humpback whale in the story and the sperm whale, are still fairly common and have a good chance of survival if they continue to be protected.

WHAT ARE THE DANGERS FOR WHALES?

Whales have been hunted by humans for many thousands of years for their meat, oil, and bones. Despite this, most kinds of whales remained quite common until recently. In the twentieth century, however, whales have been killed in enormous numbers by factory whaling ships, and many species are now threatened with extinction.

IS ANYONE HELPING WHALES?

Yes. In 1986 the International Whaling Commission, which was set up to control whaling, stopped all large-scale whaling for five years, under pressure from several conservation organizations. People who live in areas such as Greenland and Alaska are still allowed to catch a few whales, as they have done for many centuries.

ARE EFFORTS TO SAVE WHALES SUCCEEDING?

The ban on commercial whaling has allowed most kinds of whales to start increasing in number, but may have come too late for some. Unfortunately, there are countries that would like to start commercial whaling again. Many people are worried that controls proposed by the whaling countries will not be effective. Commercial whaling has driven many whale and dolphin species close to extinction. It must not happen again.

IS THERE ANYTHING YOU CAN DO?

Yes. You can write to "Save the Whales" for more information about whales and what's being done to save them.

Save the Whales
P.O. Box 3650
Washington, DC 20007

JUDY ALLEN worked in a literary agency and as a book editor before turning to writing. Her first book — a novel for children — was published in 1973. Since then she has written many books for children, including *Panda, Tiger* (a *Reading Rainbow* book), *Elephant,* and *Seal,* each a story dramatizing the plight of an endangered animal. Judy Allen wanted this story to finish on a hopeful note, despite its serious nature. She says that the ending was inspired by the fact that "in real life whales do come to each other's rescue."

TUDOR HUMPHRIES struggled to paint the tropical night waters this book requires. His problems were unexpectedly solved when he traveled to Greece and spent time diving and photographing underwater. He has always enjoyed and been involved with children, taking part in children's art festivals and teaching painting classes in grade schools. Tudor Humphries has illustrated each of the books in Judy Allen's endangered animals series.